D0127849

THE BEST OF FRIENDS

THE BEST
OF FRIENDS

Illustrated by Rosalyn White

DHARMA  PUBLISHING

© 1989 by Dharma Publishing USA. All rights reserved.
No part of this book may be reproduced in any form
without the publisher's written permission.

Library of Congress Cataloging in Publication Data
will be found at the end of this book.

Dedicated to

All the World's Children

The Jataka Tales

The Jataka Tales celebrate the power of action motivated by compassion, love, wisdom, and kindness. They teach that all we think and do profoundly affects the quality of our lives. Selfish words and deeds bring suffering to us and to those around us while selfless action gives rise to goodness of such power that it spreads in ever-widening circles, uplifting all forms of life.

The Jataka Tales, first related by the Buddha over two thousand years ago, bring to light his many lifetimes of positive action practiced for the sake of the world. As an embodiment of great compassion, the Awakened One reappears in many forms, in many times and places to ease the suffering of living beings. Thus these stories are filled with heroes of all kinds, each demonstrating the power of compassion and wisdom to transform any situation.

While based on traditional accounts, the stories in the Jataka Tales Series have been adapted for the children of today. May these tales inspire the positive action that will sustain the heart of goodness and the light of wisdom for the future of the world.

Tarthang Tulku   *Founder, Dharma Publishing*

Once upon a time in a forest there lived a Great Being in the form of a woodpecker with brilliant feathers of many colors. Not only was this bird unusually beautiful, but he was also unusually kind and intelligent. He was like a physician to the other animals, keeping watch over them and giving them good advice. So kind was his heart that he could not bring harm to any creature, and thus he lived only on berries and sweet flowers.

One day while he was flying through the darkest part of the woods, he spied a lion rolling on the ground, his mane dirty and tangled, his cries of pain pitiful and sad.

"O King of Beasts! What has happened? Have you been hit by a hunter's arrow? Have you been wounded by a buffalo's horns or an elephant's tusks? Is there any way I can help?"

"O Physician of the Forest! O beautiful bird! I have got a sharp piece of bone stuck deep in my throat, and I cannot swallow it down nor throw it up. I am in terrible agony! Please help me!"

The clever bird quickly thought of a way to aid the lion. He found a stick just the proper size, and told the lion to open his mouth as wide as he could. He then placed the stick between his top and bottom teeth to keep his jaws apart. Boldly, the physician bird entered the lion's mouth and hopped to the bottom of his throat. With his long fine beak, he gently worked the bone fragment loose and pulled it free. As he came out of the lion's mouth, he kicked away the stick, and the lion's pain was ended.

Filled with joy, the lion thanked the woodpecker again and again. And the bird was as happy as the lion, knowing that he had removed the pain of another. The happiness of others brought him great joy, and he cared not whether he was thanked or praised.

Some time later it happened that the woodpecker had been unable to find food for many days. He ached with hunger as he flew from branch to branch in search of berries or even sweet leaves. Then the woodpecker spied that very same lion beneath the trees, feasting on an antelope he had hunted down.

So hungry was the woodpecker that he wished for a morsel of the lion's meal, but he did not ask for anything. He only landed nearby and watched, hoping the lion would remember him and offer him food.

Indeed the lion recognized the woodpecker who had saved his life, but being greedy and proud, he did not understand the sweet nature of the woodpecker.

"Why should I, the mighty lion, bother with you, little bird?" he snarled. "This food is mine! Is it not enough that you are still alive after entering the mouth of a lion? I can devour anything I please. Now away with you before I lose all patience and eat you in one bite!"

The woodpecker soared straight up into the sky, showing the lion the freedom and power of birds, and speaking to the lion in the language of wings. High in the clouds, he met a sky fairy who had been watching their encounter.

"O exalted and most beautiful of birds! Why do you allow the lion to insult you? Why do you not respond with anger and revenge? You have the power to blind him in a flash with your beak or to swoop down in an instant and pluck the food from his very teeth!"

"Enough of such talk," replied the woodpecker. "The way of anger is not for me. I simply helped the lion in order to end his pain, not to gain a reward. If he chooses not to be kind in return, then I will simply leave him alone. I did not help him in order to be thanked so if he does not thank me, why should I care? It is enough that I helped my friend."

"But Great Being, why be kind to those who are not kind to you? How can you call that greedy lion your friend?"

"Kindness regards everyone as a friend, even those who do not understand kindness," replied the woodpecker. "I count as friends all those I care about — every animal in this forest is my friend. Whether one animal is kind to me one day or unkind to me another day matters not. With so many friends, there are always opportunities to bring joy to others."

"You are a true and constant friend," exclaimed the sky fairy, "for your heart never changes no matter how you are treated. How noble you are, woodpecker! How the animals must admire and love you!"

If your heart is gentle and true,

All beings will gladly trust in you.

If you count as friends everyone you meet,

Your happiness will be complete.

The Jataka Tales Series

Library of Congress Cataloging in Publication Data

The Best of friends.

    (Jataka tales series)
    Based on a tale from the Jatakas.
    Summary: Being gentle and kind, the woodpecker
helps the lion in a time of difficulty, with no thought of
thanks or reward.
    1. Jataka stories, English. [1. Jataka stories]
I. White, Rosalyn, ill. II. Series.
BQ1462.E5B47 1989   294.3'823   88-33443
ISBN 0–89800–186–2
ISBN 0–89800–187–0 (pbk.)